JUNGLE EYE

Sue Graves

Rising Stars UK Ltd.
22 Grafton Street, London W1S 4EX
www.risingstars-uk.com

 nasen

NASEN House, 4/5 Amber Business Village, Amber Close,
Amington, Tamworth, Staffordshire B77 4RP

Text © Rising Stars UK Ltd.

The right of Sue Graves to be identified as the author of this work has
been asserted by her in accordance with the Copyright, Design and
Patents Act, 1988.

Published 2009

Cover design: pentacor**big**
Illustrations: Rob Lenihan, So Creative Ltd and Paul Loudon
Text design and typesetting: pentacor**big**
Publisher: Gill Budgell
Editorial project management: Lucy Poddington
Editorial consultant: Lorraine Petersen

British Library Cataloguing in Publication Data.
A CIP record for this book is available from the British Library.

ISBN: 978-1-84680-495-3

Printed by Craft Print International Limited, Singapore

CHAPTER 1

Kojo and Sima were at Tom's flat for the evening.
They had gone there after work. They all
worked at Dangerous Games, a computer games
company, and they were good mates. Sima came
up with ideas for the games and designed them.
Kojo programmed the games. Then Tom tested
them to make sure there were no bugs.

They watched a survival programme on TV. A man called Bear was explaining how to survive in the jungle.

"He's so lucky, that bloke," said Tom.

"Not if you ask me!" muttered Sima.

"I'd love to explore jungles, like him," Tom went on. "Imagine all the animals you'd see. *And* he gets paid to do it. I'd do it for nothing!"

"Me too!" added Kojo. "It would be a real test of your survival skills."

Tom nudged Sima. "Why don't you design a jungle computer game? We could test it for real, like we've done before."

"No way!" replied Sima. "You won't catch me wading through swamps and picking beetles out of my hair. There's no way I'm ever going into a jungle — not even to test a game."

The next day, Sima arrived at the office early. She was surprised to see that Tom and Kojo were already busy at the computer.

She went over to them. They were reading about the jungle on the Internet.

"You're not still thinking about that programme we saw last night, are you?" she said.

"Yep!" said Kojo. "It was wicked!"

Tom pointed to the website. "Did you know there are millions of different kinds of plants and animals in the jungle?" he said.

"Yeah, of course I did," said Sima.

"Bet you didn't know that there can be up to 22 million ants in one colony," said Tom.

"Really?" said Sima coolly. "That's why I don't want to go into the jungle. Now let's drop the subject and get on with some work."

But Tom and Kojo talked about the jungle all morning.

At lunchtime, Kojo bought a survival skills magazine. All through lunch, he kept reading bits out to Sima.

"All right," sighed Sima, at last. "I give in. I'll design a computer game about the jungle and we'll test it for real. But I'm not making it scary! OK?"

"OK!" said Kojo. He punched the air.

Tom hugged Sima. "You're the best!" he said, giving her a kiss.

"You'd better take a look at this magazine," said Kojo. "It'll help you design the game."

Sima took the magazine. "What *have* I let myself in for?" she sighed.

Sima looked through the magazine that afternoon. She started to get interested in it.

"Did you know that you have to develop 'Jungle Eye' to move easily through the jungle?" she said.

"What's Jungle Eye?" asked Tom.

"It says here that you have to look *through* the jungle and not just in front of you," said Sima. "It makes it easier and safer to walk in a jungle if you do that. It's called Jungle Eye."

"We'll have to remember that when we test the game for real," said Kojo.

"Don't worry, it'll be easy," said Sima. "I'm not having any dangerous animals in *my* computer game."

"We'll see about that!" said Tom under his breath.

CHAPTER 2

The next day, Sima designed the game. She was really pleased with how it looked. She gave the designs to Kojo and he programmed them into the computer. By the end of the week, he had finished.

"We'll test the game tonight after work, as usual," he said.

Sima yawned and stretched. She looked at her watch. It was nearly 5.30.

"I think I'll go and get a cup of coffee while we wait for everyone to go home," she said. "Anyone else want one?"

"No thanks," said Tom.

"I'll come with you," said Kojo. "I could do with a break."

Sima and Kojo went out of the office.

As soon as they had gone, Tom went over to Kojo's computer. He put Sima's game up on screen.

"Hmmm! Looks *quite* good," he said to himself. "But I reckon I can make it a bit more exciting."

Tom opened up a new website. He downloaded pictures of dangerous animals from around the world. Then he copied them into the game.

"That's more like it," he said.

Suddenly the lights in the office flashed on and off.
It was really weird.

Pete, the IT Manager, came in.

"What's going on, Pete?" asked Tom.

"Nothing to worry about," said Pete. "Just a
power surge. We've had them before. Check
your computer's OK though. Sometimes they
can develop problems when this happens."

Tom looked at the computer. It seemed fine.
He put it on standby and waited for Kojo
and Sima.

Sima and Kojo came back a few minutes later.

"Everyone's gone home," said Sima. "Let's test the game now."

Kojo started up the game.

"Same rules as before," he said. "We all touch the screen together to enter the game. We carry on playing until we hear the words 'Game over'. Got it?"

"Yeah, got it!" said Tom and Sima.

"Hang on a second," said Tom. "You haven't explained what we've got to do in this game, Sima."

"It's a test of our survival skills," said Sima. "We've got to get to a hut in the middle of the jungle. We get points for each marker we pass on the way. We'll get a map, a compass, some matches and a rope when we enter the game."

"What sort of problems are we likely to meet?" asked Kojo.

"Not many," said Sima. "Finding our way through the jungle should be hard enough. But seriously, I think this game will be a breeze!"

Tom smiled to himself but he said nothing.

They all touched the screen together. A light flashed so brightly it hurt their eyes. They shut them tight.

CHAPTER 3

The light faded. When Kojo, Tom and Sima opened their eyes they were standing in a jungle.

They looked around them. The jungle was a tangle of enormous plants and creepers. It was gloomy and damp. They could hear strange animal noises coming from deep in the jungle.

PHEW! IT'S SO HOT AND HUMID.

59:00
THOSE ANIMALS SOUND DANGEROUS!
DON'T WORRY. THIS GAME ISN'T ABOUT DANGER. IT'S ABOUT USING OUR SKILL TO GET TO THE HUT.

Tom spotted a map and a compass nailed to a tree. Nearby was a bag which contained a rope, a bottle of water and some matches.

Tom studied the map. "Hey, this place is great," he said. "It's proper jungle! Look, these crosses show the marker posts we have to find."

He set the compass to north. Then he placed it on the map. It was hard moving through the jungle.

"You can use a stick to push back the undergrowth and test how firm the ground is," said Kojo. "I got this one off a dead tree."

WE NEED TO GO THAT WAY. COME ON, YOU TWO. GRAB THE REST OF THE STUFF AND FOLLOW ME.

"OK, Indiana Jones!" laughed Sima.

Suddenly she felt a sting on her leg.
She looked down. An huge, fat leech was
stuck on her leg. It was sucking her blood.

Tom bent down and pulled at the leech.

GET IT OFF
ME, TOM!

NO, STOP! IF YOU PULL THE LEECH OFF, SIMA COULD GET AN INFECTION. I READ ABOUT IT IN MY MAGAZINE. WE NEED TO USE A LIGHTED MATCH TO MAKE THE LEECH LET GO.

Kojo got out the matches, then lit one and held it close to the leech. It dropped onto the ground. Blood ran down Sima's leg.

They all stared at the gigantic leech. Sima shook her head. "I don't understand it," she said. "I didn't put animals like this in the game."

Tom bit his lip and looked away. He felt bad that he had put Sima in danger.

CHAPTER 4

Tom, Sima and Kojo moved on. To their relief they soon came to a tree with a white cross painted on it.

WE'VE REACHED THE FIRST MARKER POST. COME ON, THIS WAY.

STOP! DON'T MOVE.

Kojo held out an arm. They all froze.

"What's up?" whispered Sima. "I can't see anything."

"Think 'Jungle Eye'," whispered Kojo. "Look through the jungle. There's something there."

Tom and Sima looked hard through the jungle.

Then Sima let out a gasp. "It's a tiger," she hissed.

Tom went white. "But that's no ordinary tiger," he gulped. "That's *enormous*!"

QUICK, CLIMB THIS TREE. GET AS HIGH AS YOU CAN AND THEN KEEP REALLY STILL.

They threw the rope over a high branch and climbed up into the tree. The tiger came towards them. It stopped and sniffed the air. Sima, Tom and Kojo's hearts pounded as they tried not to move a muscle.

Suddenly there was a rustling sound nearby. A deer wandered out into the open. The tiger slowly crept towards it. Then it leapt and bit the deer's throat, killing it instantly. The tiger dragged its meal off into the jungle.

Sima, Tom and Kojo waited a few minutes, then slowly climbed down to the ground.

THIS IS MENTAL! WHERE HAVE THESE ANIMALS COME FROM? WHY ARE THEY SO HUGE?

THERE'S SOMETHING I NEED TO TELL YOU.

25:00

Tom hung his head. He told them how he had downloaded pictures of dangerous animals and copied them into the game. Then he explained about the power surge. "So you see," he finished, "the power surge must have made the animals bigger and even more dangerous. I'm so sorry."

"I can't believe you did that behind our backs," said Kojo. He glared at Tom. "But what's done is done. Let's get to the hut as quickly as we can. The sooner we finish this game, the better."

The three of them moved quickly and quietly through the jungle. They found the next two marker posts. A while later, they saw the hut through the trees.

THANK GOODNESS FOR THAT.

WAIT! USE YOUR JUNGLE EYES! THERE'S SOMETHING MOVING OVER THE HUT.

Tom crept closer to get a better look.

"The hut's covered with gigantic scorpions!" he said. "We've got to get to the hut before the game ends. But the scorpions are so big their stings could kill us."

Kojo checked his watch. "We're running out of time," he said. "We've got to think of something fast."

Sima had an idea. "Let's scare away the scorpions with fire," she said. "We can tie our jackets to sticks and set fire to them. Then we'll throw the burning sticks at the scorpions. Some might get burnt but the rest will run away."

"Gross!" said Kojo.

"We've no choice," said Sima. "Come on."

They gathered some dead sticks and tied their jackets around them. Kojo lit them. Then they threw them at the hut.

Sima, Tom and Kojo ran as fast as they could towards the hut.

They heard a voice saying "Game over". A bright light flashed and they shut their eyes.

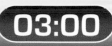

RUN TO THE HUT, FAST!

CHAPTER 5

Sima, Kojo and Tom found themselves back in the office.

"That was the worst game ever," said Sima. She looked furious. "And it's all your fault, Tom."

Tom didn't say anything. He was frozen to the spot.

"Can't you even say sorry?" Sima snapped.

Tom slowly lifted his arm. He pointed to the floor.

There, under the desk, was a giant scorpion. Its tail was dripping with poison.

"Don't move," hissed Tom. "We're all dead if this thing attacks us."

"What have we done?" whispered Sima. She was shaking with fear.

"We've got to get the scorpion back into the game world. Then we can delete the game, and the scorpion with it," said Kojo. "I've got to get to my computer to work out what to do. Don't move, Tom. Keep staring at it. I don't think it will attack unless you move."

Kojo moved slowly towards his computer. He opened up the game again. Slowly and quietly he worked on the program.

"I think this *might* work," he said at last. He backed away from the computer. "Tom, you need to get the scorpion to touch the screen."

"How do I do that, you idiot?" muttered Tom.

"Move very slowly towards the screen," said Kojo. "At the last minute, duck down behind it. The scorpion should leap at the screen to try and get you. That will send it back into the game world."

"OK," said Tom under his breath. Very slowly he moved towards the computer screen. The scorpion arched its back.

"Now!" yelled Kojo. Tom shot down behind the screen just as the scorpion leapt at him. It hit the screen. A bright light flashed and the scorpion was gone.

Quickly Kojo pressed Delete. The game disappeared from the screen.

"Thank goodness you're OK," said Sima. She gave Tom a hug.

"I'm so sorry for putting you all in danger," said Tom. "I thought I could make the game more exciting."

Sima pulled away. "Yeah well, don't think you're forgiven," she said. "You've got some serious making up to do. And next time, leave the designing to me!"

"Whatever you say!" grinned Tom.

GLOSSARY OF TERMS

bug a mistake in a computer program

colony a group of animals of the same type that live together

compass an instrument that shows which way is north

humid damp and hot

infection a disease, for example from a dirty wound

jungle thick forest in hot parts of the world

leech a bloodsucking animal

power surge a sudden flow of electricity which can damage electrical equipment such as computers

program to write a computer game or other computer program

survival skills practical know-how which helps you to stay alive in dangerous places

Quiz

1 What sort of TV programme did Tom, Sima and Kojo watch?

2 What was the man called in the TV programme?

3 What did Sima say you had to develop to move easily through the jungle?

4 What did Tom use to work out which way to go in the jungle?

5 What creature did Sima find on her leg?

6 Who got the creature off her leg?

7 What animal did the tiger kill?

8 Why were the animals in the game larger than life?

9 What animal did Tom, Sima and Kojo find in the office?

10 What was dripping from its tail?

About the author

Sue Graves has taught for thirty years in Cheshire schools. She has been writing for more than ten years and has written well over a hundred books for children and young adults.

"Nearly everyone loves computer games. They are popular with all age groups — especially young adults. But I've often thought it would be amazing to play a computer game for real. To be in on the action would be the best experience ever! That's why I wrote these stories. I hope you enjoy reading them as much as I've enjoyed writing them for you."

Answers to Quiz

1   A survival programme

2   Bear

3   Jungle Eye

4   A map and a compass

5   A leech

6   Kojo

7   A deer

8   Because of the power surge in the office

9   A giant scorpion

10   Poison